THIEF OF DRAGONS

by Gina Kammer
illustrated by Diana Renzina

STONE ARCH BOOKS
a capstone imprint

Published by Stone Arch Books, an imprint of Capstone.
1710 Roe Crest Drive
North Mankato, Minnesota 56003
capstonepub.com

Copyright © 2025 by Capstone. All rights reserved. No part of this publication may be reproduced in whole or in part, or stored in a retrieval system, or transmitted in any form or by any means, electronic, mechanical, photocopying, recording, or otherwise, without written permission of the publisher.

Library of Congress Cataloging-in-Publication Data
Names: Kammer, Gina, author. | Renžina, Diāna, illustrator.
Title: Thief of dragons / Gina Kammer ; illustrated by Diana Renzina.
Description: North Mankato, Minnesota : Stone Arch Books, an imprint of Capstone, [2024]. | Series: International School of Dragon Training | Audience: Ages 9–11. | Audience: Grades 4–6. | Summary: Toni Carpenter hates dragons, because her family home was burned down by one, but while trying to steal an egg to sell, she suddenly finds herself bonded to a young delving dragon—and that bond seems impossible to break.
Identifiers: LCCN 2023044105 (print) | LCCN 2023044106 (ebook) | ISBN 9781669067368 (hardcover) | ISBN 9781669067474 (paperback) | ISBN 9781669067405 (pdf) | ISBN 9781669067481 (epub)
Subjects: LCSH: Dragons—Juvenile fiction. | Human-animal relationships—Juvenile fiction. | Theft—Juvenile fiction. | Conduct of life—Juvenile fiction. | CYAC: Dragons—Fiction. | Human-animal relationships—Fiction. | Stealing—Fiction. | Conduct of life—Fiction.
Classification: LCC PZ7.1.K217 Th 2024 (print) | LCC PZ7.1.K217 (ebook) | DDC 813.6 [Fic]—dc23/eng/20231211
LC record available at https://lccn.loc.gov/2023044105
LC ebook record available at https://lccn.loc.gov/2023044106

Editorial Credits
Aaron Sautter, editor; Jaime Willems, designer; Whitney Schaefer, production specialist

Image Credits
Shutterstock/Marzolino, 69

Chapter 1
THE EGG THIEF 7

Chapter 2
KINDRED MAGIC 13

Chapter 3
INSIDE THE CAVES 19

Chapter 4
DRAGON SHOW PREP 25

Chapter 5
ESCAPE PLAN B 35

Chapter 6
AN UNLIKELY FRIEND 41

Chapter 7
DONE WITH DRAGONS 45

Chapter 8
STRUCK BY TRUTH 50

Chapter 9
BACK IN ACTION 53

Chapter 10
HOME 58

THE WORLD OF DRAKENKIND

Rockridge Mountains

Dragon Trainers Guild Headquarters

Rockridge Mountain Dragon Training Conservatory

Storm Country

Island School of Dragon Training

Stormy Isles

Stormy Seas

Northern Deserts

Windblast School for Dragon Trainers

Windblast Plains

Dragon Training Institute of Treefield

Treefield

International School of Dragon Training

Legends say human wizards and dragons once lived and worked together in Drakenkind. But both sides became greedy. Dragons and humans both fought over the magical gems that made them more powerful. Thus began the Gem Wars.

The wise Eternal Draken found a solution. He stripped all humans of their magic. Then he forced each dragon to bond with a human to gain one type of elemental magic. Now, the two races must work together as caretakers of their world.

Chapter 1
The Egg Thief

Of all the dragon eggs on the field, Toni spotted the one she wanted. The gemlike shell shone golden yellow in the sun. It wasn't the flashy ruby red or sapphire blue of others. No one would notice Toni as she slipped in behind the other kids to grab it. They were too busy finding their own eggs to bond with. But Toni wasn't there to bond with a dragon. She wanted to steal an egg to sell it.

The arena was packed with students' parents. They hoped to see their 10-year-olds become Kindred—those who are bonded to dragons. But Toni's parents weren't there. They thought Toni was staying with her cousin. They would never guess that she had sneaked into the International School of Dragon Training.

In fact, until recently, this was the last place Toni wanted to be. She hated dragons. A year ago, dragons had burned down her home. But now, she was going to get back at them. Once she had this egg, she could sell it to a traveling merchant she knew. Then she'd have enough money to do whatever she wanted. Her family could rebuild. They wouldn't have to stay with friends while they figured things out. She could be home again.

Toni looked around quickly. No one said anything as she stepped around the dozens of eggs scattered in the grassy arena. She paused and studied a few eggs on the way, just like the other kids were doing.

Suddenly, Toni jumped as a nearby Windblast girl with wild hair squealed. The diamond-like egg at her feet flashed with light. Toni stared. The melon-sized eggshell shattered into sparkling dust. In its place stood a wyvern the size of a bear!

Huh, thought Toni. *I guess the bond does give dragons magic.* She'd heard that the first burst of magic between dragon and Kindred was powerful. Still, she didn't think it happened so fast.

Toni shook her head. *Focus, Toni!*

She took a big step over a row of eggs to get to the golden-yellow egg. She hoped her bag would be big enough to hold it. Treefielders often carried large bags. She planned to grab the egg, stuff it in the bag, and walk away with a sad face. Sometimes kids didn't find a match with any eggs. Toni would pretend that was what happened to her. Then she'd make her escape.

"Lady Sparkles!" the Windblast girl yelled out her new dragon's name. The parents and teachers clapped.

While everyone was cheering, Toni crouched over her egg. She opened her bag and stretched out her hand to shove in the egg. She glanced back to make sure no one was looking.

Good, she thought. *The wyvern is blocking the crowd. No one will see.*

FLASH!

Toni quickly turned back to the egg. It was glowing brightly. She shaded her eyes.

What? No! No, no, no . . . Toni breathed quickly. She felt a zap of energy through her body. It felt warm and somehow . . . right?

This isn't happening! Toni had to get out of there. Fast. She stepped backward. But she tripped over another egg and landed with a thud on the ground.

In front of Toni, the yellow gemlike egg burst open. Bits of the shell glittered as they fell around her. There, in the egg's place, was a stocky dragon with little wings. It snuffled her soft boot, making the horn on its snout wiggle.

Toni scooted back. "No!" She hissed. "Get away!"

The dragon stretched its thick neck. With a quick nip, it snatched Toni's brimmed hat.

"Hey!" Toni grabbed for the hat and missed.

Just then, a shadow fell over Toni. *"Ahem,"* said a disapproving voice. "And who might you be?"

Toni glanced up at a short woman dressed in black. She held a black parasol in one hand. Her other fist was on her hip as she leaned in toward Toni. "You're not supposed to be here, are you?"

"Uh, I, uh . . ." Toni stammered. She watched the woman's laced boot tapping quickly. She had to be a rider from the Rockridge Mountains. But she looked so proper in her skirts and corset. Toni's stomach sank. No. This wasn't any Ridge Rider. She was a Ridge Rider *professor*. That was the worst combination.

Toni had been caught.

Chapter 2

Kindred Magic

Toni groaned.

"I'm Toni," she whispered as the dragon snuffled her feet.

"Well, Toni," said the woman, "I'm Professor Chambers. It looks like you've become a Kindred. You've matched with this delving dragon. You sparked his inner magic. Now it's your duty to train and care for him."

Toni let the professor's words sink in. *Kindred. Magic.* She couldn't believe it. She was bonded to . . . a *dragon?* No! Toni felt sick.

Professor Chambers closed her parasol and pointed it at Toni's wool hat and coat. "You're a Treefielder, right? A delving dragon will be very helpful for the fields and plants. It's a good bond. Isn't that why you're here?"

Toni swallowed and looked at the ground. She said nothing.

"Interesting," the professor said with a raised brow. "So, you were going to leave him behind?"

Toni looked away. She clenched her hands, ripping out fistfuls of grass.

Chambers popped her parasol open over her head. "As I see it," she said, "you have two choices. You can join the International School of Dragon Training. Here you can fulfill your bond with this delving dragon. Or, I will bring you to the Council."

Toni's eyes widened. She didn't want to be in trouble with the Council. Or her parents.

She thought quickly. She would have to play along. At least long enough to steal another egg to sell. She couldn't give up.

Toni sighed and nodded. "I'll join the school."

Chambers raised her chin toward the crowd and other kids. "Good. Then you'd better name your dragon."

Toni jerked her head up. "Name? But . . ."

Chambers looked at Toni hard. The dragon stuffed his snout into Toni's hat. It caught on his horn, and he snorted.

Toni took a quick breath. "Um, right. Ah . . . *Snuffles?*"

"Is that a question?"

"No, professor."

"Snuffles it is." Chambers flicked a small notebook and pen out of a pouch on her belt. She began writing notes.

Around her, Toni heard other kids chatting and laughing. Parents were patting the kids' backs and wishing them well at school. But nobody was cheering for Toni.

"I'll get you enrolled and recorded,"

Professor Chambers said. "For now, you can join Hana and Lady Sparkles to get settled."

Toni blinked. *Did Chambers just say "Lady Sparkles" as if the dragon was like any other student?*

"You and Hana will room in the Cliffside tower. The caves for delving dragons and wind wyverns are near Cliffside. The fifth-years will show you around." Chambers took a breath. "Now, I must get ready to give the opening speech."

"Speech? Wait, you mean the one the school president gives?" Toni felt like she was falling even though she was sitting on the ground.

The president of the International School knew that Toni had snuck in. She would need to escape with an egg—and fast. Before Chambers tracked down her parents and told them where she was. She knew her parents would make her stay with her cousin for good.

Chambers tipped her hat to Toni. Then she whistled sharply and called out, "Soot!"

Gusts of air soon beat down. Toni glanced up to see a pitch-black fire drake spreading his claws overhead. She quickly pinched her eyes shut. Seeing the drake sparked a flash of memory. Suddenly, Toni recalled searing hot flames in a storm. Her heart raced. Then she heard a soft thud.

Toni opened one eye to see the big dragon land before Chambers. He lowered himself down to let Chambers climb onto his back.

"I'll see you with the other first-years at the opening." Chambers said it like an order.

Toni just twisted her rope belt in her hands and nodded.

The fire drake crouched, gave a beat of his wings, and sprang into the air. Toni watched in awe as their dark outline soared over the arena wall.

Chapter 3

Inside the Caves

A moment later, something soft touched Toni's hand. She glanced down. Snuffles was nudging her hat toward her.

Toni grabbed her hat and smashed it down over her messy hair. She stood and glared at Snuffles. "This is all your fault, you know."

Snuffles just blinked and twisted his head to one side.

"Ugh! Why am I even talking to you? I won't be here long anyway. Then you can go do . . . whatever dragons do. Without me."

Snuffles bumped his hard snout on her leg.

"*What do you want?*" Toni almost shouted.

Someone giggled behind Toni. She turned to see the Windblast girl, Hana. Her wind wyvern looked over her shoulder.

"He's just hungry!" she said, smiling. "All newly hatched dragons are. C'mon! Let's get them to their caves."

"Um, yeah. That's probably it," Toni mumbled. She just wanted to get away from the young dragon. But as she turned and walked out of the arena with Hana, she heard Snuffles's little grunts and snorts follow right behind her.

As they walked the narrow strip of land connecting the arena to the campus, Toni thought about running. But the sea crashed against the cliffs lining either side of the path. There was nowhere to run. Besides, it seemed Snuffles would follow her until he got food. Sighing, Toni let Hana chatter as they walked.

"So where are you from?" Hana asked.

Toni raised an eyebrow. Could Hana really not tell? Most everybody on Drakenkind wore

distinct clothing from their nation. Storm Watchers were easy to spot with their cloaks and beaded hair. Ridge Riders had dark furs and leather clothes. Windblasts almost all had goggles and long coats.

"I'm from a small Treefield village not far from here," Toni answered.

"Oh, wow!" said Hana. "That's lucky you're so close! I live in one of the northern canyons. It's about as far from here as you can get."

The school's main grounds were ahead, with wide arches and towers. They were built right into the mountainside.

"That's Cliffside ahead of us," Hana said, pointing to their left. The tower rose high up on the cliff face.

"Can't wait!" Toni said, forcing a smile. She just wanted to get this over with.

As they followed the other first-years, Toni saw the school staff carrying the unbonded eggs back to the caves. Her mind raced with ideas of how to get one.

"Oh! Toni, look! Here are two caves close together," Hana said. "Let's choose these so our dragons can be friends!" She led Lady Sparkles into the first one.

"There's already food here!" Hana called out.

"That's perfect," Toni said. "Go on. Get in there." She pointed toward the cave, and Snuffles went right in.

Free of the squat dragon, Toni peeked into the other cave. She saw Hana arranging some rocks and colorful gems inside. Toni sneaked past the cave entrance and raced down the tunnel.

Deeper inside the mountain, Toni hid behind a large rock until she saw a staff member leave a cave. She tiptoed to the cave and peeked around the corner. Inside she saw a ruby egg. This was her chance! Toni slipped her bag over her head and knelt on the stone.

"Oy! You, there. Are you lost?" a man's voice called.

Toni jerked away from the egg. She spun around to see a man in a guard's uniform. "Uh, yeah. I guess so. Where are the caves for the new dragons?" She played along, looking around with wide eyes.

"Hmph," said the guard suspiciously. "You went too far. Go back up that tunnel, first-year. You won't miss them."

Toni nodded and snatched her bag from the cave floor. Gritting her teeth, she headed back to Hana so they could find their own room in the tower.

Chapter 4

Dragon Show Prep

The next few days felt like one of Drakenkind's biggest whirlwind storms to Toni. A fifth-year student, Bint, showed her to her classes. He also took her and Hana to Tinker Town, a mazelike group of workshops and markets under the school. There, dragon trainers could find everything needed to make magical gadgets, including gems filled with dragon magic. Trainers used their gadgets and the special gems to help their dragons direct their magic.

Toni traced the runes marked on a gadget shaped like a folded fan. "It's for changing air currents," Bint said. The beads in his hair clicked together as he turned toward her. "I'm still working on it, but it's nearly ready. I'll test it again with my wind wyvern tomorrow."

Toni nodded, but she didn't care about the gadgets. She was focused on finding a way to trick the guards. It wouldn't be easy. They watched the dragon eggs closely.

"What do the runes do?" Hana asked.

"They're said to be the language of the old wizards. They're supposed to direct the magic and tell it what to do," he replied.

Toni perked up. She had an idea. Maybe a gadget could help her steal an egg. "Can we use the gadgets without our dragons?" she asked.

Bint laughed. "No, of course not. We can fill the gems with dragon magic to help them. But only dragons have magic."

Toni's hopes fell. She'd have to learn to train her dragon after all. She didn't like it, but she'd have to use him to steal an egg. Once she finally had one and sold it, she'd be done with dragons forever.

"Come on, we need to practice for midterms! Will you come with me this time?" Hana begged Toni a few weeks later.

Toni rolled her eyes. The midterm dragon show was still a month away. She didn't get why everyone was making such a big deal about it.

Hana frowned. "Plus, you can't keep ignoring Snuffles. He misses you."

Toni snorted. "No, he doesn't. He's just a dragon."

Hana gasped. "*Just* a . . . how could you say that?"

"No, not . . . " Toni winced. "I just meant . . . you know."

"Um, no," said Hana. "I don't."

"Oh. Well, uh," Toni stumbled over her words. "Forget it. You're right. Let's go. I do need to work with Snuffles more."

Hana smiled. "That's better!"

Toni *had* started paying attention in her classes. But she still didn't like dragons. She didn't want to spend more time with them than she had to. However, it was hard to avoid them with midterms coming up.

Toni led Snuffles out of his cave, where he'd been napping. They followed Hana and Lady Sparkles across the campus green, past the huge Old Dragon. It was always there, but Toni still couldn't tell what kind it was. It looked like a mix of every type of dragon. It snored softly in a curled heap.

"I told our group to meet us in the arena," Hana said. "Kili, Dom, and Rett should already be there."

"What about Lill?" Toni asked. The first-years

were split into groups of six—one student for each dragon type. Lill had the storm serpent.

"Lill is sick today."

"That's too bad," Toni replied. She kind of liked Lill. The Storm Watcher girl was quiet but smart. Plus, she didn't ask Toni so many questions.

"How will we practice without her?" Toni asked as they walked. They needed everyone to finish all the midterm tasks. Students would get certain items to use, such as a rock and a seed. Together, they had to use the items and work with their dragons, and their dragons' magic, to achieve their goals.

Hana shrugged. "We can still practice other things. We just won't have Bubbles's rain magic today."

Kili, Dom, and Rett were riding their dragons in a game of fly tag when they arrived at the arena. "Let's start!" Hana called. They landed in front of her.

"I found this sunflower seed to practice a planting task. And we can pretend that rock is one of our items," Hana said, pointing.

Hana was always the group leader. Other kids listened to her. Toni felt a surge of pride. But she swallowed it down. She didn't want to like these people. She would be leaving soon. Very soon. She had to think of her family first. She couldn't make friends.

"Hey, Toni, turn this rock into something we can use for dirt!" Dom said.

"Okay, we're up, Snuffles," said Toni, climbing onto his back. She put a loop of rope over his horn. Glowing gems were braided into it. "You know what to do! *Delve!*"

At the command word, Snuffles shoved his horn against the large boulder. Toni held tightly as Snuffles lurched forward. The rock crumbled into a pile of gravel. Then Snuffles shoved his snout into it to make a little hole.

"Now, Rett!" Hana said.

Rett glided over with his leaf lizard. They dropped the seed into the hole.

"What do we do for water?" Rett asked.

They all looked at Kili.

"Don't look at me!" Kili said. "My dragon only controls sea water. I don't think a tree would like saltwater."

Dom scratched his head. "I have water in this bottle. You know," he said, cringing, "in case Sparky, um, *sparks,* again."

Everyone nodded. Dom was still working with his fire drake to control his lightning abilities.

"Let's try it," said Hana.

Dom poured the water on the seed. "It's all yours, Rett!"

Rett and the leaf lizard used a gadget that looked like a small pitchfork with gems on each tine. Rett stuck it in the dirt.

"*Sprout,*" Rett commanded. The leaf lizard

bit the handle of the fork, and the gems on the gadget glowed.

Nothing happened.

"It's still too rocky," Rett said.

Toni frowned. "On it!" She patted Snuffles on his back, and he stepped forward. Toni switched to a gadget that looked like a clump of gems tied together. It wasn't finished. She wasn't a good tinkerer. But it would have to do. She quickly scratched a rune onto the gadget and tied it to Snuffles's horn.

"Uh, *dirt*," Toni commanded.

Snuffles turned his head back to look at her. They hadn't practiced using his magic like that yet.

"What?" she said, frowning. "Just try it."

Snuffles turned back and put his horn to the pile of crumbled rock like before. The clump of gems glowed brightly. Then the pile turned to dirt and dust.

"Good?" Toni asked Rett.

He shrugged and tried his dragon's magic again. This time, a thick, green stem shot up from the ground.

"Woohoo!" Dom cheered.

"Yes!" said Hana.

Even Toni had to grin at the quickly growing sunflower.

Chapter 5

Escape Plan B

A couple of weeks later, the whole school was buzzing. Everyone was getting ready for the midterm dragon show. But not Toni.

Today would be Toni's best chance to get a dragon egg. The dragon caves were nearly empty. Only the tunnel to the eggs was blocked off. Still, Toni knew how she could get an egg and get away unseen.

She hurried toward Snuffles's cave. This time, she knew she wouldn't fail. She'd been working on her plan for weeks.

"Toni! Great. You're here. The group is getting ready," Hana said as Toni rounded the bend near Lady Sparkles's cave.

Toni slid to a stop. She breathed hard.

"Oh," said Toni, licking her lips. "Well, I . . ." she trailed off. She thought quickly. "I wanted to practice some delving with Snuffles. We still need to work out some kinks with the new gadget."

Hana put a finger to her cheek. "Hmm, true . . . you do need to work on that. Okay. But don't be too long, yeah?"

"You got it," said Toni, ducking into Snuffles's cave. She waited until she heard the wings of Hana's dragon scraping along the walls. They were gone.

"Okay," Toni told Snuffles. "We're going to, umm, *practice* for the midterm here in the caves."

She felt silly. Snuffles wouldn't understand. He was just a dragon. "Right. Whatever. Come on," she said, waving her hand.

Toni led Snuffles to a tunnel above the lower caves. He sniffed her hand.

"You want this?" Toni showed him a large carrot, his favorite veggie treat. "All you need to do is delve straight down." She pointed. "Got it?"

Snuffles waited while Toni climbed onto his back. She looped the braided rope gadget over his horn. "*Delve!*" she commanded.

Within seconds, they broke through into the cave below. Luckily, Snuffles caught the edge of the hole with his claws before they fell.

"Yes!" Toni hopped off the dragon's back and looked over the edge. "Good work, Snuffles."

He gave her a toothy grin.

"Fetch!" Toni threw the carrot as far as she could. "Then go home!"

Snuffles knew "go home" meant to go back to his cave. Toni gave him one final scratch behind his horn. He made a low grumble and closed his eyes. Then he lumbered off.

He'll be fine, Toni told herself, feeling a pang

of guilt. But it quickly passed. She didn't need this dragon. She didn't need any of them. She just needed one of the eggs glittering in the dark below. She took a deep breath.

Toni lowered herself down and dropped through the little hole. "Oomph!" She hit the bottom hard. It was a long drop.

She stood up and shook off the dust. There, glittering in the middle of the cave was a sapphire egg. Toni lifted it with both hands. It was heavy. She dropped it into her bag. Yes! She'd finally done it!

Toni looked up. The hole above was the only exit. But it was too far for her to reach. She looked around in the dim light. There were no large rocks she could stand on to reach the hole.

Then she heard a scratching sound from above. Toni's stomach flipped. Was it a guard? She peered up through the hole. A familiar snout and horn poked through.

"Snuffles! What are you doing here?"

Rocks began raining down. Snuffles used his claws to make a bigger hole. Toni backed up. Then Snuffles dropped through.

Snuffles looked at the spot where the egg had been. Then he looked at Toni's bag. For the first time, Toni feared what Snuffles might do. But he only waddled up to her. He waited for her to hop on his back like he always did.

"You're—you're helping me?" Toni asked him, confused.

Once she was on, she whispered, *"Delve!"* And Snuffles did.

Chapter 6

An Unlikely Friend

When they finally broke through into the last cave tunnel, Toni saw where they were. They were at the mountain tunnel entrance to the school. Snuffles had helped her escape!

Toni stared at Snuffles. Snuffles twisted his neck and stared back at her.

"You knew all along," she said. "And you're still helping me."

Snuffles huffed and lowered his head.

Toni scrambled off Snuffles's back. Feelings of guilt stabbed at her. She looked back at the entrance. There were no guards. This was her chance to escape.

As Snuffles turned to leave, a tear slid down Toni's cheek. She ran back to Snuffles. She wrapped her arms around his thick neck.

"You've been the best friend," Toni sobbed. She hadn't realized it before. But she knew now how much she truly loved her dragon.

Toni knew she should run while she had the chance. But she couldn't leave Snuffles behind. She didn't know what to do.

Toni then heard laughter and a woman's voice at the school entrance. The guards were back. It was too late. She couldn't get away now.

But the egg was still hidden in Toni's bag. She could find a way to sneak it out and sell it later. First, she needed to hurry back to the arena. Her group would fail the midterms if she didn't show up. Toni hadn't forgiven dragons and Trainers for destroying her family's home. But she still didn't want her classmates to fail.

"Shh!" Toni warned Snuffles as they turned around. "Hurry, we need to get back. Fast."

When Toni dashed through the arena arch, Lill spotted her first. "Hey, where have you been?" Her storm serpent, Bubbles, floated next to her.

Toni shrugged. The heavy egg in her bag hit against her leg. She felt another pang of guilt. *The egg!* In her rush to help her friends, she hadn't thought about what to do with the egg. She couldn't bring it to the midterm show. Someone would discover it.

"Uh, no time to explain now," Toni said. "I have to go. I forgot to bring our new gadget!" It wasn't exactly a lie. She didn't have it. She had to return to her room. Then she could hide the egg and get her gadget at the same time.

"Ugh, Toni!" Lill said. "You'd better be quick!"

Toni nodded. "Take Snuffles!" She handed his rope to Lill, then ran off toward Cliffside Tower. The heavy egg weighed her down as she ran.

Chapter 7

Done with Dragons

Toni took a shortcut through Central Tower. She held her bag in both hands, trying to hide the egg's shape. As she ran down an empty hallway, she heard someone say her name.

Toni slid to a stop. She tried to quiet her breathing and crept up to an office door. Inside, Professor Chambers's back was turned. She was speaking to someone.

"Yes, it was the Carpenter family home. Soot and I volunteer for Emergency Aid. But we were useless in that storm. I'm afraid we did more harm than good. Soot's blast burned their home completely."

Toni took a sharp breath. *It was Professor Chambers's dragon that burned my home!* She couldn't believe it. Chambers had helped her. She hadn't reported Toni to the Council. Toni had almost started to like the professor—a Dragon Trainer!

Toni stumbled away from the office. She turned and ran back the way she'd come. She needed to get out of the school. She knew she should never have trusted dragons or their trainers.

Swiping at her eyes with her fists, Toni burst through the main doors and onto the school green. She knew she had to get out of there. She shouldn't have waited so long. Quickly, she came up with a new plan. She would find a way through the mountains and away from this awful school on her own.

Toni ran toward the nearby lake. She could follow the water to get away, right? She hoped it was a good plan. It had to be.

"There she is! Toni! Hey, Toni!" Hana was running across the green with Rett and Lill. Snuffles ran with them, using his little wings to help carry him along.

Toni tried to ignore them. She kept running.

"Hey, stop! Where are you going?" Hana caught up to Toni, and she paused. "We were wondering if you needed help. Did you find your gadget?" Hana hooked her finger in Toni's bag and peered in.

Toni froze.

Hana gasped. Rett and Lill looked in too.

"Toni . . ." Lill said softly. "What are you doing with an *egg*?"

"I'm stealing it, okay?" Toni shot back. She glared at them hard. "I'm leaving you all. I don't care if you fail. Dragon Trainers are nothing but a sham!"

The three stood staring at her, eyes wide. Snuffles lowered his head to his feet. Behind

them, in the center of the green, the Old Dragon raised his head. He looked straight at Toni with piercing eyes. Toni shivered.

"You'll never get away with this," Lill said in a low voice.

"You won't make it out," Rett said.

With tears in her eyes, Hana whispered, "But you'd be leaving Snuffles behind. How could you?"

Toni looked away to hide her own tears. "I . . . I hate dragons," she said with a breaking voice.

One by one, Toni's group, her only friends, turned and left her. They headed back to the arena. Snuffles gave her one last nudge with his nose. Then he turned his back on her too.

Chapter 8

Struck by Truth

Toni turned and ran without really watching where she was going. At the lake shore, she stumbled up the rocky path at the mountain's base.

Toni had nothing. She had no home. And now she had no friends. She had only the heavy egg.

Toni's bag caught on the edge of a rough rock. It pulled her off balance. She fell and scraped her knee. When she looked up, she saw the mountain rise far above her. Without Snuffles to create a tunnel, Toni would never reach the other side. But she knew he'd never help her again.

Toni put her face in her hands. She hadn't gained anything by taking the egg. Instead, she'd lost everything.

"Oh, Snuffles!" Toni cried. "What have I done?" Toni coughed, sobbing. She had been so wrong.

Toni rolled onto her back. Her tears streamed down her face. She'd been far better off as a dragon trainer. She was Kindred! What was she thinking? She could have used her training to help her family. Instead, she was just a thief.

Toni sat up. She realized the truth. Stealing a dragon egg wouldn't really help her get control over her life. For true strength, she needed to help others.

"I'll turn myself in," Toni said to herself. Her feelings of guilt were fading away. "I'll return the egg. But not until I help my friends."

Toni raced back to the arena. The Old Dragon watched her cross the green to the walkway. As she did, he nodded slightly, then lowered his head and closed his eyes. Toni shivered again. But this time it wasn't from fear. She knew she was doing what she was meant to.

Chapter 9

Back in Action

In the arena, Toni sneaked behind the seats until she found her group. They were out on the field—and doing terribly. Hana was trying to get Snuffles to delve. She pointed at a boulder. But without Toni there, Snuffles struggled to use his magic. He just made tiny, random holes in the arena floor.

Toni jogged onto the field. The professors judging the group began to whisper among themselves. Her friends paused to watch her.

Toni jogged up to Snuffles and put her forehead on his. "I'm so sorry, Snuffles," she said softly. "I'm never going to leave you again."

Like the good and loyal dragon he was, Snuffles gave her his toothy grin. He snuffled her hair.

Toni smiled. "I don't deserve you." Then she hopped onto Snuffles's back and shouted, "*Delve!*"

Snuffles turned toward the boulder, lowered his head, and blasted the rock to fine dust.

"Well, don't just stand there!" Hana yelled. "Rett, get that tree growing! We need to feed these dragons!" She looked at Toni. "That's our task. We have to figure out how to feed all of them. We got one boulder and an acorn, and except for Kili, we can't leave the arena."

Toni raised an eyebrow. They knew their task for the dragon show would be a surprise. But she hadn't thought it would be so hard.

Hana chewed on her lip. "We're starting with the plant-eating dragons. We can grow plants. At least we've practiced that. Although, not with trees . . ."

Rett poked the acorn into the dry dirt from the boulder. Lill rode in on Bubbles, showering rain on the spot. Rett used his fork gadget and the leaf lizard's magic to grow a tiny tree. Then it stopped. Hana groaned.

But Toni was a Treefielder. She knew trees and knew just what to do.

"Lill!" Toni called. "More rain! Keep it raining! Rett needs help!"

Lill nodded and directed Bubbles's rain magic over the tree. It kept growing bigger and bigger.

Hana gathered the others. "That will feed the plant eaters. But now what? I still haven't figured out how we're going to feed the meat-eating dragons."

Toni rubbed her head. Ocean waves crashed over and over again around the arena. The sea gave Toni an idea. Hana had said they couldn't leave the arena. But Kili could. Maybe they could still bring something into the arena. "What about fish?"

"How?" asked Kili.

"Can you bring up fish in a wave?" Toni asked.

Kili nodded. "But how do we get it into the arena?"

Toni looked at Hana. "Can you and Lady Sparkles make a big whirlwind?"

Hana smiled. She knew what Toni had in mind. "Yes! We've been practicing."

"Great! Then let's get to work," Toni said, grinning.

Toni and Snuffles dug a large bowl shape in the dirt. Kili and her sea serpent skimmed over the sea's surface. They soon created a large wave full of fish. Hana and her wind wyvern were ready with their whirlwind. It sucked up the fish and water. Then they moved the fish over the arena wall and dropped them into Toni's dirt bowl.

The meat-eaters quickly caught the fish with their claws. Dom and Sparky cooked the fish with a quick blast. While the meat-eaters ate the fish, the leaf lizard and storm serpent munched the tree leaves. All the dragons ate well.

The group cheered. "We actually did it!" said Hana, laughing. She hugged Toni. "Thank you! Thanks for coming back. We couldn't have done it without you."

Toni's group headed to the campus green with the other first-years to celebrate. They had passed the midterms. More importantly, Toni finally felt happy to be at the school.

Chapter 10

HOME

Back at the main school grounds, Toni quietly slipped away. She went back to Professor Chambers's office and knocked on the door.

"Come in!" Chambers called. When Chambers saw Toni enter, she held out her hand. Toni pulled the sapphire egg out of her bag. Looking at the floor, she handed it to Chambers and waited.

Chambers didn't say anything. Instead, she handed Toni a folded letter. Toni saw it was from her parents. She gulped.

Her parents were very angry. Their letter scolded her for lying to them and not going to her cousin's home like she was supposed to do.

Toni looked up at Professor Chambers. "Did you know all along?"

Chambers just shrugged. She set the egg on her desk.

"You did know," Toni said. "And you didn't try to stop me?"

"I was keeping an eye on things. But I hoped you would make the right choice. You did have me a bit worried at the end." Chambers gave her a crooked grin.

"I had to do some homework though. I discovered what happened during the storm last year." Chambers's smile fell. She looked serious. "I'm so sorry. The fire was an accident. Soot and I were the closest to your village. We wanted to help, but we couldn't do much in that storm. When a tree blew down, Soot panicked. He blasted it with fire. Unfortunately, your home burned with it."

Toni listened, shocked. Her throat felt tight. Her eyes stung with tears.

"I want you to know, Atonia, I'm making things right for your family," Chambers said quietly. "They'll get the help they need. And you can continue here at school. But only if you promise to use your skills to help—not to harm."

Toni nodded vigorously. She swiped her eyes quickly. "Yes. I will!"

"Well then, you'd better get to the party. I think someone's waiting for you . . ." Chambers's eyes twinkled.

Toni felt a huge wave of relief as she left the professor's office. Then, just as she stepped through the door, she was knocked off her feet. Something very powerful had tackled her. Then she felt something snuffle in her hair. Toni reached up and wrapped her arms around Snuffles's thick neck. "Yes, I'm still here. I'm not going anywhere. I love you too."

All this time, Toni wanted to go home. But now she realized, she was *already* home.

The Dragons of Drakenkind

Fire Drakes

Magical Element: fire

Abilities: may breathe fire, lightning, smoke, and even static electricity

Appearance: spiked ridges over the head and spikes down the back and tail; dark-colored scales with red markings around the eyes and a light-colored underbelly; dark, large, leathery wings; four legs with five sharp claws on each foot

Egg: ruby-red eggshells

Diet: meat-eater, but will not eat raw food

Location: mainly found in the Rockridge Mountains

Cultural Origin: these fiery reptiles are inspired by the fearsome, fire-breathing dragons in legends and tales from medieval Europe

Wind Wyverns

Magical Element: air

Abilities: controlling wind and air currents

Appearance: narrow bodies with two large, powerful wings; two strong hind legs with clawed feet; claws at the tips of wings used like front feet to help move on land; covered with colorful feathers; typically smaller than other dragons; they have extra winglike extensions on their tails used to help steer while flying at high speed

Egg: clear diamond eggshells

Diet: meat-eaters, mostly land animals

Location: mainly live on the Windblast Plains

Cultural Origin: these colorful, feather-covered reptiles are inspired by the mythological gods of the ancient Mayan and Aztec religions, such as the god Quetzalcoatl

Sea Serpents

MAGICAL ELEMENT: water bodies

ABILITIES: controlling water in oceans, lakes, rivers, seas, swamps, or ponds

APPEARANCE: long snakelike bodies with larger bellies and longer necks; shimmering, fishlike scales; feathery, frondlike gills; webbed claws; some have wings like a flying fish to fly short distances; can survive on land, but spend most of their time underwater

EGG: blue sapphire eggshells

DIET: meat-eaters, mostly fish

LOCATION: mainly found around the Stormy Isles

CULTURAL ORIGIN: these water dragons are inspired by sea serpents from ancient Greek myths and the legendary Watatsumi from Japan

Storm Serpents

Magical Element: precipitation

Abilities: power to produce rain, mist, snow, frost, or dew

Appearance: long, snakelike bodies; no wings; four legs with four birdlike claws on each foot; staglike horns; fine furlike feathers with longer tufts like a mane; mustaches; a gem (its reformed eggshell) worn on its head or carried in a claw that lets it fly

Egg: light to dark purple amethyst eggshells

Diet: eats both meat and plants

Location: mainly live in Storm Country

Cultural Origin: these wingless, magical dragons are inspired by the Chinese Loong and Korean Yong dragons

Delving Dragons

Magical Element: earth

Abilities: controlling soil, rock, and sand

Appearance: sturdy bodies with tiny yet hard glittery scales; small wings that allow them to fly a short distance; short horns on their snouts help them dig through earth and rock; slow moving, but have a powerful and poisonous bite; two rows of spiked ridges along their backs that merge at the tail

Egg: golden-brown to yellow-orange topaz eggshells

Diet: mostly meat-eaters, but with some plant roots

Location: mainly found in Treefield with a few in the Windblast Plains

Cultural Origin: these two-legged reptiles find their inspiration in the serpentlike lindworm beasts from Norse and Central European myths

Leaf Lizards

Magical Element: plant life

Abilities: influencing growth and health of plants

Appearance: softer spikes with leathery scales in a variety of leafy colors and patterns; flat, leaf-shaped bodies, tails, and wings

Egg: green emerald eggshells

Diet: mostly plant-eaters, but also eat some insects

Location: mainly live in Treefield, with a few in the Windblast Plains

Cultural Origin: these multi-headed dragons are partially inspired by the Hydra, a multi-headed monster from ancient Greek lore

Lindworms in Ancient Mythology

Snuffles, the delving dragon in the world of Drakenkind, is inspired by and similar to legendary creatures called lindworms. These mythical beasts are found in several ancient tales from Central Europe and Norse mythology. Lindworm means *serpent* or *dragon* in old languages.

Lindworms are often described as dragons with two front legs and a curled tail. Occasionally, they may have two small wings, but they're normally wingless in most stories. They slither along like a snake, with help from their front legs. Lindworms don't breathe fire. But they usually have a poisonous bite or breath.

A statue and fountain of the Klagenfurt lindworm was built in the 1500s.

Local legends in Klagenfurt, Austria, tell of a lindworm that caused problems in the area when the city was founded. Eventually, the local duke hired knights to capture and kill the beast. The dragon eventually became a symbol for the city.

In an epic tale called the Volsunga Saga, a lindworm called Fafnir guards his treasure. In the Norse Eddas, the mythology of the Norse gods, lindworms include one named Nidhogg. This wicked creature chews on the roots of Yggdrasil, the World Tree.

In Swedish folklore, lindworms can swallow their tails to roll like a wheel. In one Danish fairy tale, Prince Lindworm is half man and half snake. When he eventually sheds his skin, he is fully human.

Talk About It

1. In Drakenkind, dragons hatch when they are bonded with a human. If you could bond with a dragon, which type do you think would hatch for you? Why?

2. Toni makes some bad choices in this story. But she tries to make things right. Have you ever made a mistake that hurt someone you care about? What did you do to fix things?

Write About It

1. Toni has a hard time letting go of her anger toward dragons. Write about a time you were angry about something. How did you handle it?

2. Drakenkind has several types of dragons. Make up a new dragon of your own. Describe what it looks like, its abilities, and where it would live.

Glossary

arena (uh-REE-nuh)—a large area or building with seating for sports or entertainment events

bond (BAHND)—to form a close relationship with someone; in Drakenkind, dragons and human trainers form a strong, magical connection to each other.

campus (KAM-puhs)—the land and buildings of a school or university

delve (DELV)—to dig

gadget (GA-jit)—a mechanical or magical device or tool used to help do something

green (GREEN)—an open grassy area in a central place such as on a college campus or a town square

market (MAR-kit)—a place where people can buy, sell, or trade items

runes (ROONS)—symbols or characters used for writing an ancient language; runes in Drakenkind have magical qualities.

About the Author

GINA KAMMER loved dragons growing up. She never outgrew them. Instead, she went on to study them in mythologies, medieval texts, and other literature at college and universities. Now she's an author, editor, and book coach specializing in science fiction and fantasy. She also teaches writing courses at inkybookwyrm.com. Her other interests include tea, traveling, oil painting, archery, and snuggling her grumpy bunny. She lives among piles of books in Minnesota with her husband and daughter. Find her at ginakammer.com.

About the Illustrator

DIANA RENZINA was born in 1989 in Riga, Latvia, where she grew up and lives today. She is mostly a self-taught artist, but she has been studying digital design at a local university that has helped her understand how to make projects, not just random pictures. She has worked for a couple of creative agencies as a full-time illustrator as well. Her two main sources of inspiration are folklore and nature.